Pour Oscar et Maminou Meeow
S.B.

First American edition published in 2009 by Boxer Books Limited.

Distributed in the United States and Canada by Sterling Publishing Co., Inc.
387 Park Avenue South, New York, NY 10016-8810

First published in Great Britain in 2009 by Boxer Books Limited.
www.boxerbooks.com

Text and illustrations copyright © 2009 Sebastien Braun

The rights of Sebastien Braun to be identified as the author and
illustrator of this work have been asserted by him
in accordance with the Copyright, Designs and Patents Act, 1988.

The illustrations were prepared using hand-painted line shapes which were digitized and assembled, then colored.
The text is set in Helvetica.

ISBN 978-1-906250-86-7

1 3 5 7 9 10 8 6 4 2

Printed in China

All of our papers are sourced from managed forests and renewable resources.

Meeow
and the big box

Sebastien Braun

Boxer Books

This is Meeow.

Meeow is a black cat.

Hello, Meeow!

This is Meeow's big brown box.

Meeow carries the big brown box.

You're strong, Meeow!

Meeow likes
the color red.

Meeow has some red paint.

Meeow paints the

big brown box red.

Good job, Meeow!

Meeow is going to cut a hole in the big red box with his scissors.

Be careful, Meeow!

Well done, Meeow!

Meeow has a
big green block,

a little orange chair,
and a blue mug.

Meeow climbs on the chair, then the block. He puts the blue mug on the big red box.

What can Meeow be making?

Meeow puts
the chair in
the big red box.
Then Meeow
climbs in.

Nee-naw!

Nee-naw!

Meeow has made his very own fire engine.

Clever Meeow!

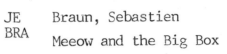

266 1847